編者的話

很多同學問，如何才能學好英文文法呢？讀了那麼多文法書，為什麼還不會？我認為，**學好文法，最簡單的方法，就是做練習題，遇到不會做的題目再查文法書**。這樣，題目愈做愈有興趣，考試時會寫，英文文法也通了。

一般文法書的練習題，都是從名詞、動詞開始分類，照這樣分類，會使讀者限於狹窄的範圍，容易猜到答案，題目做到後面，前面又忘記了，對文法沒有全面性的了解，最糟的是，很快就會失去興趣，放棄文法。

本書共有 50 回測驗題，每回測驗只有 10 題，讀者做了會很有成就感，每回測驗都是一個挑戰，看自己進步了多少。本書每條題目，都是從國內外大規模考試中，整理出來的，文法題考來考去，其實都是這些類似的題目。在本書中，我們刻意將文法規則打散，均勻分佈在每回測驗中，如果做了哪一條題目不會，可以看本書的自修本，也可查閱「**文法寶典**」，務必徹底了解。

英文要學好，一定要學會文法，文法是一種歸納，把公認為最好的語言表達方法，歸納成規則，這樣子，我們說出來的話或寫出來的句子，就不會有錯誤。但是，規則也有很多例外，往往例外的、特殊的，也就是常考的，只要讀通這本書，不僅考試會考，你的英文文法，也會有相當的程度。

這本書另附有自修本，每條題目都有詳細解答，對錯答案都有明確交代，每句都有中文翻譯及文法分析。句中單字、成語均有註釋，一目了然，一看就懂。

劉 毅

碰到題目不會做，怎麼辦？看自修本的詳
解，再不懂，查閱「文法寶典」。還不懂，直
接打電話給劉毅老師。

劉毅老師文法解答專線：0933-940-727

TEST 1

Directions: *Of the four choices given after each sentence, choose the one most suitable for filling in the blank.*

1. If I _____ the truth, I would tell you.
   - (A) know
   - (B) have known
   - (C) knew
   - (D) will know   (   )

2. This is _____ house for such a small family.
   - (A) too big
   - (B) too big a
   - (C) too a big
   - (D) big too a   (   )

3. Jack was caught _____ on the exam.
   - (A) cheat
   - (B) cheated
   - (C) cheating
   - (D) being cheated   (   )

4. Eric is _____ tennis player on his team.
   - (A) the much best
   - (B) very the best
   - (C) much the better
   - (D) by far the best   (   )

5. You cannot be _____ when choosing friends.
   - (A) too careful
   - (B) more careful
   - (C) so much careful
   - (D) too much careful   (   )

6. I would _____ see the movie. It's too violent.
   - (A) not rather
   - (B) rather not
   - (C) rather not to
   - (D) like not to   (   )

7. You shouldn't have bothered, Mrs. Owens; you're _____ to me.
   - (A) much too kind
   - (B) too much kind
   - (C) very much kind
   - (D) very too kind   (   )

8. Mary is a good cook, and _____.
   - (A) so I do
   - (B) so do I
   - (C) so I am
   - (D) so am I   (   )

9. When she has a lot of homework, she burns the midnight oil more often than _____.
   - (A) not
   - (B) none
   - (C) ever
   - (D) never   (   )

10. Two of these three students can speak English; _____ cannot.
    - (A) another
    - (B) other
    - (C) the other
    - (D) the others   (   )

TEST 2

Directions: *Of the four choices given after each sentence, choose the one most suitable for filling in the blank.*

1. Foreign tourists are often surprised at the _____ prices of things in Tokyo.

    (A) big
    (B) high
    (C) much
    (D) expensive   (   )

2. _____ the medicine, and your pain will go away.

    (A) If you take
    (B) Take
    (C) Taken
    (D) Taking   (   )

3. We will go camping this weekend _____ it rains or not.

    (A) whether
    (B) which
    (C) unless
    (D) though   (   )

4. These kinds of books are _____ little value.

    (A) having
    (B) of
    (C) with
    (D) without   (   )

5. Our company offers _____ workweek, competitive salary and attractive benefits.

    (A) five-day
    (B) five-days
    (C) a five-day
    (D) a five-days   (   )

6. _____ what I had ordered, I called the mail-order company.

    (A) Received not

    (B) Not received

    (C) Not having received

    (D) Not to receive   ( )

7. Bill's car is nicer than _____ of my brother.

    (A) one

    (B) that

    (C) it

    (D) which   ( )

8. He could not _____ from smiling, though with a slight sense of guilt.

    (A) avoid

    (B) help

    (C) refrain

    (D) quit   ( )

9. There are a _____ of dolphins.

    (A) herd

    (B) flock

    (C) swarm

    (D) school   ( )

10. The opera starts at seven. We _____ be late.

    (A) needn't

    (B) mustn't

    (C) don't have to

    (D) haven't got to   ( )

TEST 3

Directions: *Of the four choices given after each sentence, choose the one most suitable for filling in the blank.*

1. If you were really interested in what I'm saying, you _____ staring out of the window.
   (A) will be
   (B) will have been
   (C) would have been
   (D) wouldn't be   ( )

2. The question _____ at today's meeting is whether we should postpone the plan till next month.
   (A) discussing
   (B) is discussed
   (C) to be discussed
   (D) to be discussing   ( )

3. She's going to _____ her father into buying a new car.
   (A) say
   (B) speak
   (C) talk
   (D) tell   ( )

4. A violent demonstration must be avoided by _____ means.
   (A) no
   (B) all
   (C) some
   (D) none   ( )

5. Tom _____ breakfast at seven in the morning.
   (A) is having always
   (B) always is having
   (C) has always
   (D) always has   ( )

6. _____ will be the next president of the United States of America?

   (A) Do you think who
   (B) Who do you think
   (C) Who do you know
   (D) Whom do you think   (   )

7. Now that I have a motorcycle, I _____ ride my bicycle.

   (A) seldom never
   (B) ever seldom
   (C) hardly ever
   (D) hardly never   (   )

8. There is _____ when the patient will regain consciousness.

   (A) not to tell
   (B) no telling
   (C) not telling
   (D) only telling   (   )

9. He mentioned a book _____ I can't remember now.

   (A) which title
   (B) with the title which
   (C) in which the title
   (D) the title of which   (   )

10. The performance was so outstanding that the audience gave the musician a _____ ovation.

    (A) stand
    (B) stands
    (C) stood
    (D) standing   (   )

TEST 4

Directions: *Of the four choices given after each sentence, choose the one most suitable for filling in the blank.*

1. You should prepare everything for tomorrow before you _____ to bed.
   - (A) go
   - (B) going
   - (C) will go
   - (D) are going   (   )

2. There was a drunken man _____ on his back in the street.
   - (A) laid
   - (B) lain
   - (C) lying
   - (D) laying   (   )

3. _____ do you think the population of San Francisco is?
   - (A) How
   - (B) How many
   - (C) How large
   - (D) How much   (   )

4. He didn't finish his homework, and _____.
   - (A) either did I
   - (B) so did I
   - (C) I didn't, too
   - (D) I didn't, either   (   )

5. Father gave me an expensive watch of Swiss _____ as my birthday present.
   - (A) make
   - (B) made
   - (C) makes
   - (D) making   (   )

6. The businessman was leading _____ to spend weekends with his family.

   (A) a life so busy
   (B) too busy a life
   (C) so a busy life
   (D) such busy a life   (   )

7. We haven't decided _____ to go to the movies or to go to the baseball game tonight.

   (A) if
   (B) which
   (C) where
   (D) whether   (   )

8. _____ in a very difficult situation, the doctor never had any rest.

   (A) Work
   (B) Working
   (C) Worked
   (D) To work   (   )

9. If I _____ about his illness, I would have visited him at the hospital.

   (A) know
   (B) have known
   (C) had known
   (D) might have known   (   )

10. They had a civil ceremony at the courthouse and the judge pronounced them _____.

    (A) husband and wife
    (B) a husband and a wife
    (C) the husband and the wife
    (D) the husband and his wife   (   )

TEST 5

Directions: *Of the four choices given after each sentence, choose the one most suitable for filling in the blank.*

1. All things _____, Mr. Smith is a very good husband.
   - (A) considered
   - (B) considering
   - (C) having considered
   - (D) to be considered ( )

2. Some are _____ his plan, while others are against it.
   - (A) as
   - (B) for
   - (C) with
   - (D) alike ( )

3. My younger brother has to serve in the military _____ beginning in September.
   - (A) two years ago
   - (B) for two years
   - (C) since two years
   - (D) during two years ( )

4. I'm sorry, but I forgot _____ the magazine you wanted.
   - (A) to buy
   - (B) buying
   - (C) of buying
   - (D) to have bought ( )

5. Who _____ has read Shakespeare's beautiful poems can forget their fascination?
   - (A) that
   - (B) which
   - (C) who
   - (D) whom ( )

6. This rose does not smell as sweet as _____ I bought the other day.

    (A) the one
    (B) it
    (C) such
    (D) which   (   )

7. One of my sisters is a lawyer; _____ are both doctors.

    (A) others
    (B) another ones
    (C) the others
    (D) some others   (   )

8. Jason regrets _____ harder when he was in college.

    (A) not to have studied
    (B) not having studied
    (C) having not studied
    (D) of having not studied   (   )

9. The mountains of Nepal are much higher than _____ of Japan.

    (A) those
    (B) this
    (C) these
    (D) that   (   )

10. Many TV talk shows are _____ programs.

    (A) life
    (B) live
    (C) alive
    (D) lived   (   )

TEST 6

Directions: *Of the four choices given after each sentence, choose the one most suitable for filling in the blank.*

1. _____ luck would have it, I was at home when he called.

   (A) As
   (B) If
   (C) When
   (D) Unless   (   )

2. There were beautiful willow trees on _____ side of the river.

   (A) nor
   (B) both
   (C) any
   (D) either   (   )

3. We cannot _____ see the star with the naked eye.

   (A) help
   (B) necessarily
   (C) hardly
   (D) scarcely   (   )

4. I know little of mathematics, _____ of physics.

   (A) still less
   (B) much more
   (C) rather more
   (D) more or less   (   )

5. The juvenile delinquent denied _____ the motorcycle.

   (A) to steal
   (B) of stealing
   (C) having stolen
   (D) to have stolen   (   )

6. Superstition has _____ that a black cat going across your path will bring you bad luck.

    (A) it
    (B) so
    (C) to
    (D) such   (   )

7. _____ with the wind and the rain, the game was spoiled.

    (A) How
    (B) What
    (C) Which
    (D) Why   (   )

8. We are going on a hike tomorrow, _____.

    (A) weather to permit
    (B) weather permitting
    (C) weather permits
    (D) for weather to permit   (   )

9. He did nothing _____ weep when he heard of his mother's death.

    (A) but
    (B) as
    (C) that
    (D) to   (   )

10. There are quite a _____ interesting things to see in this city.

    (A) many
    (B) number
    (C) few
    (D) much   (   )

TEST 7

Directions: *Of the four choices given after each sentence, choose the one most suitable for filling in the blank.*

1. I recognized him at once, as I had seen him _____.
   - (A) since
   - (B) before
   - (C) ago
   - (D) forward   (   )

2. The price of the house is now _____ it used to be.
   - (A) three times as high as
   - (B) as three times high as
   - (C) three times as expensive as
   - (D) as three times expensive as   (   )

3. _____ teaching French at college, Mr. Peterson teaches a class at a high school.
   - (A) His
   - (B) Beside
   - (C) Besides
   - (D) In addition   (   )

4. Certain medicines, _____, will turn out to be harmful.
   - (A) excessively used
   - (B) excessive using
   - (C) having excessively used
   - (D) having excessively been used   (   )

5. _____ records were imported from Germany.
   - (A) Almost
   - (B) Most of
   - (C) The most
   - (D) Almost all the   (   )

6. Five minutes earlier, _____ we could have caught the last train.

    (A) or
    (B) but
    (C) and
    (D) so   (   )

7. Linda is _____ more beautiful than Helen.

    (A) very
    (B) much
    (C) by far the
    (D) far and away the   (   )

8. Kate speaks English very fast. I've never heard English _____ so quickly.

    (A) speak
    (B) speaking
    (C) spoken
    (D) to speak   (   )

9. Two thirds of the work _____ finished.

    (A) are
    (B) did
    (C) is
    (D) will   (   )

10. A language may extend _____ national and cultural boundaries.

    (A) on
    (B) in
    (C) out
    (D) beyond   (   )

TEST 8

Directions: *Of the four choices given after each sentence, choose the one most suitable for filling in the blank.*

1. She _____ be over thirty; she must still be in her twenties.

    (A) may
    (B) must
    (C) oughtn't
    (D) can't   (   )

2. _____ they will win the game in the end.

    (A) No doubt
    (B) Not doubt
    (C) No doubtfully
    (D) Not any doubt   (   )

3. Mr. White gave me _____ little money he had then.

    (A) as
    (B) that
    (C) what
    (D) which   (   )

4. I _____ stay poor than become rich by dishonest ways.

    (A) would better
    (B) would more
    (C) would rather
    (D) would like to   (   )

5. My stand _____ what it is, I have to oppose this idea.

    (A) alone
    (B) being
    (C) off
    (D) on   (   )

6. Come what _____, she will not give up.

    (A) can
    (B) may
    (C) must
    (D) should   (   )

7. Work is not the object of life _____ than play is.

    (A) more
    (B) less
    (C) any more
    (D) anything more   (   )

8. We had a number of trees in our yard _____ down by the strong wind.

    (A) blow
    (B) blown
    (C) to blow
    (D) being blown   (   )

9. Students can't learn _____ facing some hardships.

    (A) but
    (B) whether
    (C) without
    (D) except for   (   )

10. It is common knowledge that cheese _____ milk.

    (A) makes
    (B) is made into
    (C) is made of
    (D) is made from   (   )

TEST 9

Directions: *Of the four choices given after each sentence, choose the one most suitable for filling in the blank.*

1. The man whose head had been shot was as _____ as dead.

   (A) good
   (B) well
   (C) much
   (D) ever   (   )

2. Let's walk a little faster _____ we should be late for school.

   (A) fear
   (B) unless
   (C) lest
   (D) so that   (   )

3. The day was rainy, and _____ was worse, it was stormy.

   (A) so
   (B) such
   (C) what
   (D) which   (   )

4. That is the restaurant _____ the Italian food was extremely good.

   (A) that
   (B) which
   (C) at which
   (D) on which   (   )

5. _____ that in August, 1984, my work obliged me to go to Japan.

   (A) Happening was
   (B) That happened
   (C) I happened
   (D) It happened   (   )

6. No sooner _____ begun his speech than he felt dizzy.
   - (A) John has
   - (B) has John
   - (C) John had
   - (D) had John   (   )

7. He is much happier now than _____.
   - (A) ever before
   - (B) never before
   - (C) before ever
   - (D) before never   (   )

8. _____ on the hill, the church commands a fine view.
   - (A) Standing
   - (B) Situating
   - (C) Laying
   - (D) Locating   (   )

9. Never in all my life _____ such a beautiful sunset.
   - (A) saw I
   - (B) I have seen
   - (C) have I seen
   - (D) I did see   (   )

10. He felt something cold _____ his right leg.
   - (A) touched
   - (B) to touch
   - (C) touching
   - (D) to have touched   (   )

TEST 10

Directions*: Of the four choices given after each sentence, choose the one most suitable for filling in the blank.*

1. _____ Mr. Smith, have you seen him lately?

   (A) Talking
   (B) Talking of
   (C) To talk
   (D) To talk about   (   )

2. I tried to take the dog out of our house, but he _____ go out.

   (A) were to
   (B) had to
   (C) might not
   (D) would not   (   )

3. _____ on the farm all day long, he was completely tired out.

   (A) Worked
   (B) Not working
   (C) Being working
   (D) Having worked   (   )

4. The baseball game had _____ started when it began to rain.

   (A) sooner
   (B) rarely
   (C) seldom
   (D) scarcely   (   )

5. You mustn't miss _____ this wonderful movie.

   (A) in seeing
   (B) seeing
   (C) to have seen
   (D) to see   (   )

6. Kevin loves to play golf among _____ .
    (A) another thing
    (B) other things
    (C) other's things
    (D) the other things   (   )

7. It was so cold this afternoon that _____ anybody went
    swimming.
    (A) all
    (B) almost
    (C) hardly
    (D) most   (   )

8. I am no _____ able to operate this machine than he is.
    (A) far
    (B) much
    (C) very
    (D) more   (   )

9. My father is said to _____ really hard in his youth.
    (A) work
    (B) have worked
    (C) be working
    (D) be worked   (   )

10. We suffered from _____ troubles.
    (A) great many
    (B) greatly many
    (C) a great many
    (D) many a great   (   )

TEST 11

Directions: *Of the four choices given after each sentence, choose the one most suitable for filling in the blank.*

1. Remember _____ I've just told you. It'll be very important when you grow up.

    (A) as
    (B) that
    (C) what
    (D) which   (   )

2. _____ by the sound of the door, I checked to see who it was.

    (A) Startle
    (B) Startled
    (C) To startle
    (D) Startling   (   )

3. The ten-year-old boy cannot so _____ as sign his name.

    (A) far
    (B) good
    (C) long
    (D) much   (   )

4. He stole, _____ to get things for himself as to get a thrill from it.

    (A) as well
    (B) not rather
    (C) not so much
    (D) for as much   (   )

5. Everything in the universe is _____ matter or energy.

    (A) either
    (B) neither
    (C) whether
    (D) whatever   (   )

6. Please include a self-addressed, stamped envelope if you would like the photos _____.

  (A) return
  (B) returned
  (C) returning
  (D) to return   (   )

7. Statistics _____ a required course for majors in economics.

  (A) are
  (B) is
  (C) are being
  (D) is being   (   )

8. If the sun _____ in the west, she would marry you.

  (A) rises
  (B) risen
  (C) was to rise
  (D) were to rise   (   )

9. She is always _____ the ball.

  (A) to miss
  (B) missed
  (C) missing
  (D) being missed   (   )

10. He is good at reading, but his listening ability is _____ average.

  (A) below
  (B) beyond
  (C) behind
  (D) within   (   )

TEST 12

Directions: *Of the four choices given after each sentence, choose the one most suitable for filling in the blank.*

1. I have never seen such a good dancer. She is really _____.
   - (A) anybody
   - (B) anything
   - (C) something
   - (D) everyone   (   )

2. Health is above wealth, for _____ can't bring us so much happiness as _____.
   - (A) this, that
   - (B) that, this
   - (C) these, those
   - (D) those, these   (   )

3. _____ to it that such a thing does not happen again.
   - (A) Do
   - (B) Mind
   - (C) See
   - (D) Watch   (   )

4. The audience gave the singer a big hand. _____, he tried to express his thanks.
   - (A) Deeply moved
   - (B) Having been moving
   - (C) Having moved
   - (D) Moving   (   )

5. Jack seldom, _____, goes to church on Sundays.
   - (A) if any
   - (B) if ever
   - (C) if anything
   - (D) if necessary   (   )

6. Jeff and Jenny saved _____ they could to visit their uncle in Hawaii.

   (A) as a lot of money as
   (B) as much money as
   (C) money as a lot as
   (D) money as possible as   (   )

7. He had to carry _____ from his house to the station.

   (A) much luggage
   (B) so many luggages
   (C) three pieces of luggages
   (D) many luggage   (   )

8. What is it _____ you really want to say?

   (A) what
   (B) how
   (C) that
   (D) where   (   )

9. _____ seems easy at first often turns out to be difficult.

   (A) It
   (B) That
   (C) What
   (D) Which   (   )

10. I spent the last few days _____ those historic sites.

   (A) visit
   (B) visited
   (C) visiting
   (D) to visit   (   )

TEST 13

Directions: *Of the four choices given after each sentence, choose the one most suitable for filling in the blank.*

1. _____ stay indoors? It's raining outside.

    (A) Why
    (B) Why not
    (C) How about
    (D) How come   (   )

2. Make sure that the sick _____ properly attended.

    (A) are
    (B) has
    (C) is
    (D) will have   (   )

3. He told me his father was an astronaut, _____ was hard to believe.

    (A) it
    (B) that
    (C) what
    (D) which   (   )

4. There was a sign at the lake, which said, "_____."

    (A) No fish
    (B) Not to fish
    (C) No fishing
    (D) Not fishing   (   )

5. I wonder why Steven avoided _____ Kelly yesterday.

    (A) to meet
    (B) meeting
    (C) from meeting
    (D) having met   (   )

6. _____ he be given another chance, he would make efforts to become a good student.

    (A) If
    (B) When
    (C) Might
    (D) Should   (   )

7. Are there any good films _____ this week?

    (A) about
    (B) by
    (C) on
    (D) out of   (   )

8. Her sister bought three _____ of stockings yesterday.

    (A) pieces
    (B) pairs
    (C) lumps
    (D) tubes   (   )

9. I was called into the office first, my name _____ at the head of the list.

    (A) holding
    (B) putting
    (C) making
    (D) being   (   )

10. Students should try _____ late.

    (A) not be
    (B) to not be
    (C) to don't be
    (D) not to be   (   )

TEST 14

Directions: *Of the four choices given after each sentence, choose the one most suitable for filling in the blank.*

1. The old American didn't know that Singapore is a country _____ to the south of Malaysia.

   (A) lain
   (B) lying
   (C) to lie
   (D) which is lying   (   )

2. Honestly speaking, my income is _____ but as large as you think it is.

   (A) nothing
   (B) anything
   (C) something
   (D) everything   (   )

3. He _____ neglect his duty.

   (A) ought to not
   (B) ought not to
   (C) ought not
   (D) not ought to   (   )

4. _____ hearing the news, she burst into tears.

   (A) Into
   (B) On
   (C) To
   (D) At   (   )

5. _____ you speak about my husband in that disgusting way!

   (A) What for
   (B) How about
   (C) How dare
   (D) How would you say   (   )

6. Tony called on Mary _____ to find that she was away for the vacation.

   (A) as
   (B) until
   (C) only
   (D) before   (   )

7. If I _____ to college at that time, I would be a more successful businessman now.

   (A) go
   (B) went
   (C) have gone
   (D) had gone   (   )

8. _____ what to say, she remained silent.

   (A) Doesn't know
   (B) Knowing nothing
   (C) Not known
   (D) Not knowing   (   )

9. This is the place _____ I saw him last night.

   (A) that
   (B) which
   (C) what
   (D) where   (   )

10. Five kilometers _____ a long way if people have to walk.

    (A) are
    (B) is
    (C) was
    (D) were   (   )

TEST 15

Directions: *Of the four choices given after each sentence, choose the one most suitable for filling in the blank.*

1. Why on _____ did you sell your newly-built house?
   - (A) earth
   - (B) place
   - (C) reason
   - (D) ground   (   )

2. Since he needed to sign the document, he asked me if I had anything _____.
   - (A) to write
   - (B) to write with
   - (C) to be written
   - (D) to writing on   (   )

3. You are the _____ person I would have expected to see here.
   - (A) surprising
   - (B) rare
   - (C) least
   - (D) last   (   )

4. Your cell phone is really small, _____ with mine.
   - (A) to compare
   - (B) comparing
   - (C) if compare
   - (D) compared   (   )

5. Never _____ of meeting you here in Taipei.
   - (A) I dreamed
   - (B) did I dream
   - (C) dreamed I
   - (D) I did dream   (   )

6. Although it was raining heavily this morning, the rain finally let _____ in the afternoon.

   (A) on
   (B) up
   (C) off
   (D) out   (   )

7. I'll have finished my homework by the time the TV program _____.

   (A) starts
   (B) will start
   (C) have started
   (D) will have started   (   )

8. She promised _____ the next chance go by.

   (A) not him to let
   (B) him not to let
   (C) him not letting
   (D) to him to let   (   )

9. There is no possibility of Mary _____ the bar exam.

   (A) to pass
   (B) passing
   (C) will pass
   (D) have passed   (   )

10. Scholars agree that the variety of wildlife is nowadays less than _____ used to be.

   (A) those
   (B) it
   (C) they
   (D) ones   (   )

TEST 16

Directions: *Of the four choices given after each sentence, choose the one most suitable for filling in the blank.*

1. _____ Michael looks tired; he stayed up all night.

   (A) There is wonder
   (B) It's no wonder
   (C) It's the reason for
   (D) This is reasonable   (   )

2. What do you say _____ a visit to the Palace Museum?

   (A) to pay
   (B) paying
   (C) to paying
   (D) having   (   )

3. _____ you have to do is sit down and stay calm.

   (A) All
   (B) Only
   (C) How
   (D) Which   (   )

4. He saw a girl _____ in blue.

   (A) dressed
   (B) dressing
   (C) being dressed
   (D) dressed herself   (   )

5. There is no mother but _____ her children.

   (A) loves
   (B) love
   (C) loving
   (D) loved   (   )

6. The shopkeeper was busy _____ the customer and didn't notice that the boy was about to shoplift.

    (A) serving
    (B) to serve
    (C) to serve to
    (D) with serving   (   )

7. This is the very book _____ I wanted to buy.

    (A) that
    (B) what
    (C) how
    (D) when   (   )

8. Though he has a Ph.D. in archaeology, he is not _____ of an archaeologist.

    (A) more
    (B) much
    (C) less
    (D) little   (   )

9. The teacher had hardly finished the class _____ Jimmy rushed out of the classroom.

    (A) after
    (B) when
    (C) as
    (D) where   (   )

10. Cindy was made _____ all the dishes after the dinner.

    (A) wash
    (B) washed
    (C) washing
    (D) to wash   (   )

TEST 17

Directions: *Of the four choices given after each sentence, choose the one most suitable for filling in the blank.*

1. It will be _____ spring when you get to London.
   - (A) late
   - (B) lately
   - (C) last
   - (D) latest   (   )

2. He was very nervous because he _____ in public.
   - (A) didn't use to speak
   - (B) didn't used to speak
   - (C) wasn't used to speaking
   - (D) wasn't used to speak   (   )

3. She does not seem to be _____ of guessing others' feelings.
   - (A) enabled
   - (B) possible
   - (C) able
   - (D) capable   (   )

4. _____ this letter find you well and happy!
   - (A) I am afraid
   - (B) I think
   - (C) May
   - (D) Will   (   )

5. If I were _____ go abroad, I would go to France.
   - (A) on
   - (B) to
   - (C) about
   - (D) for   (   )

6. I remember _____ him at this place two years ago.

   (A) to see
   (B) seeing
   (C) to seeing
   (D) to be seen   (   )

7. It was stupid _____ him to say such a thing to the teacher.

   (A) with
   (B) of
   (C) as
   (D) to   (   )

8. Although intonation is seldom taught in some language courses, it is _____ important for communicating accurately.

   (A) all the more
   (B) none the less
   (C) none the worse
   (D) much more   (   )

9. It _____ him millions of dollars to buy the villa in the countryside.

   (A) spent
   (B) cost
   (C) took
   (D) made   (   )

10. You _____ go to bed as stay up doing nothing.

   (A) should
   (B) had better
   (C) would rather
   (D) might as well   (   )

TEST 18

Directions: *Of the four choices given after each sentence, choose the one most suitable for filling in the blank.*

1. We are different _____ that you like crowds and I don't.
   - (A) so
   - (B) of
   - (C) at
   - (D) in   (   )

2. I would rather _____ at home myself than eat out.
   - (A) cook
   - (B) cooking
   - (C) to cook
   - (D) to cooking   (   )

3. Tom has _____ for modern painting.
   - (A) an eye
   - (B) the eye
   - (C) eyes
   - (D) the eyes   (   )

4. Rome is a city worth _____.
   - (A) visit
   - (B) to visit
   - (C) visiting
   - (D) to visiting   (   )

5. If only you _____ to the movies with me last night!
   - (A) would go
   - (B) went
   - (C) had gone
   - (D) go   (   )

6. How come _____ such a lie?
    (A) he told
    (B) did he tell
    (C) has he told
    (D) was he to tell   (   )

7. We regret _____ you that you are to be dismissed next week.
    (A) tell
    (B) to tell
    (C) told
    (D) to telling   (   )

8. He used to _____ to school every morning.
    (A) walk
    (B) walking
    (C) being walked
    (D) having walked   (   )

9. I saw a beautiful lady sitting with her legs _____.
    (A) crosses
    (B) crossed
    (C) crossing
    (D) to cross   (   )

10. _____, he could speak confidently in public.
    (A) Being mere child
    (B) Mere child as he was
    (C) A mere child as he was
    (D) Though he was mere child   (   )

TEST 19

Directions: *Of the four choices given after each sentence, choose the one most suitable for filling in the blank.*

1. Relax. The angrier you get, _____ you become.
   - (A) the uglier
   - (B) more ugly
   - (C) ugly person
   - (D) the more ugly   (   )

2. You should know _____ than to lend him money. He will never repay you.
   - (A) best
   - (B) better
   - (C) well
   - (D) fine   (   )

3. My mother insisted _____ up smoking.
   - (A) me giving
   - (B) I gave
   - (C) on my giving
   - (D) on I should give   (   )

4. The question is which _____.
   - (A) choose
   - (B) to choose
   - (C) choosing
   - (D) chosen   (   )

5. _____ you have formed a bad habit, it is difficult to get rid of it.
   - (A) Until
   - (B) Unless
   - (C) Before
   - (D) Once   (   )

6. They are so _____ that it is difficult to tell which is which.

   (A) alike
   (B) likely
   (C) nearly
   (D) same   (   )

7. It _____ me two hours to find your new house.

   (A) cost
   (B) took
   (C) spent
   (D) occupied   (   )

8. Roughly _____, this is correct.

   (A) speak
   (B) spoke
   (C) speaking
   (D) to speak   (   )

9. He _____ sometimes go mountain-climbing with his friends when young.

   (A) used
   (B) should
   (C) would
   (D) is used to   (   )

10. Such _____ the case, I can't let you go.

    (A) is
    (B) doing
    (C) being
    (D) done   (   )

TEST 20

Directions: *Of the four choices given after each sentence, choose the one most suitable for filling in the blank.*

1. I was so _____ that I fell asleep before the film ended.
   (A) bored
   (B) boring
   (C) bore
   (D) boredom   (   )

2. It is necessary _____ the traffic rules.
   (A) you following
   (B) your following
   (C) of you to follow
   (D) for you to follow   (   )

3. Please write in ink, and don't forget to write _____ every other line.
   (A) at
   (B) from
   (C) in
   (D) on   (   )

4. The new medicine saved me from an illness which might _____ have been fatal.
   (A) therefore
   (B) still
   (C) otherwise
   (D) instead   (   )

5. Both of them are very brilliant, but _____ warm-hearted.
   (A) neither of them is
   (B) neither one of them are
   (C) none of them is
   (D) none of them are   (   )

6. _____ the air conditioner, the summertime would be unbearable.

    (A) Were it for
    (B) If it were not
    (C) If were it not
    (D) Were it not for   (   )

7. There are two reasons for our decision, and you know one of them. Now I'll tell you _____.

    (A) another
    (B) other
    (C) the other
    (D) the others   (   )

8. The doctor gave me _____ on how to keep fit.

    (A) much advices
    (B) many advices
    (C) a few advice
    (D) a great deal of advice   (   )

9. Please lock the door when you _____.

    (A) leave
    (B) will be leaving
    (C) will have left
    (D) will leave   (   )

10. Of these two opinions, I prefer the _____ to the former.

    (A) late
    (B) last
    (C) later
    (D) latter   (   )

TEST 21

Directions: *Of the four choices given after each sentence, choose the one most suitable for filling in the blank.*

1. She has to study _____ two years before she graduates.

    (A) more
    (B) another
    (C) other
    (D) much   (   )

2. Mary didn't want to walk at night on her own _____ something terrible should happen to her.

    (A) so that
    (B) unless
    (C) despite the fact that
    (D) for fear that   (   )

3. I know nothing about Roy _____ he is a college student.

    (A) excepting
    (B) except for
    (C) except from
    (D) except that   (   )

4. The doctor is a great authority _____ children's diseases.

    (A) on
    (B) in
    (C) of
    (D) over   (   )

5. If they had surrendered, we _____ them.

    (A) shouldn't kill
    (B) needed not to kill
    (C) didn't have killed
    (D) needn't have killed   (   )

6. The discussion the villagers had on the environment was quite
    _____.

    (A) alive
    (B) lived
    (C) lively
    (D) living   (   )

7. My father objected to _____ like an invalid.

    (A) treat
    (B) treating
    (C) be treated
    (D) being treated   (   )

8. I don't know _____ to consult with.

    (A) what
    (B) when
    (C) where
    (D) whom   (   )

9. As the French enjoy their wine, _____ the Chinese enjoy their
    tea.

    (A) as
    (B) so
    (C) such
    (D) like   (   )

10. A: Does Jack live in the suburbs or in the center of the city?
     B: _____ I know, he lives near the center.

    (A) As far as
    (B) As long as
    (C) As much as
    (D) So long as   (   )

TEST 22

Directions: *Of the four choices given after each sentence, choose the one most suitable for filling in the blank.*

1. The sun rises _____ the east.
    - (A) to
    - (B) in
    - (C) at
    - (D) under   (   )

2. _____ you were a singer, what kind of song would you like to sing?
    - (A) Suppose
    - (B) Supposed
    - (C) Supposition
    - (D) Supposedly   (   )

3. It is a pity that nobody was saved in the accident, _____ it?
    - (A) does
    - (B) doesn't
    - (C) was
    - (D) isn't   (   )

4. The _____ fans rushed onto the stage during the concert.
    - (A) excite
    - (B) excited
    - (C) exciting
    - (D) excitement   (   )

5. Nancy studied hard _____ flunk calculus again.
    - (A) so as to
    - (B) as not to
    - (C) so as not to
    - (D) not so as to   (   )

6. He didn't come to work for some reason or _____.

   (A) other
   (B) another
   (C) others
   (D) the other   (   )

7. Charles has _____ better days and finds it difficult to live only on his pension.

   (A) removed
   (B) known
   (C) reminded
   (D) thought   (   )

8. As soon as he entered the village, he found himself _____ curious children.

   (A) surrounding
   (B) surrounded by
   (C) surrounding by
   (D) to be surrounding   (   )

9. We considered _____ but finally decided against it.

   (A) go
   (B) to go
   (C) going
   (D) about to go   (   )

10. Jane decided _____ the man she met in Paris.

   (A) to marry
   (B) marrying to
   (C) to marry with
   (D) to get married   (   )

TEST 23

Directions: *Of the four choices given after each sentence, choose the one most suitable for filling in the blank.*

1. He was _____ to give me a ride home.
   - (A) as kind
   - (B) more kind
   - (C) so kind as
   - (D) enough kind   (   )

2. All _____ there were some 250 passengers on our flight.
   - (A) said
   - (B) told
   - (C) talked
   - (D) mentioned   (   )

3. 11/16 is read as _____.
   - (A) eleven sixteen
   - (B) eleventh sixteen
   - (C) eleven sixteenth
   - (D) eleven sixteenths   (   )

4. We _____ them at football yesterday.
   - (A) won
   - (B) failed
   - (C) beat
   - (D) lost   (   )

5. My friend _____ I supposed would pass the examination has failed.
   - (A) who
   - (B) whom
   - (C) of whom
   - (D) as   (   )

6. _____ in plain English, the book was easy to read.

   (A) Written
   (B) Writing
   (C) To write
   (D) Having written   (   )

7. Eric and Frank, _____ is my boyfriend, went to the party with me.

   (A) both of whom
   (B) either of which
   (C) either of them
   (D) neither of whom   (   )

8. At the party, I had my photograph _____ by a friend of mine.

   (A) take
   (B) taken
   (C) to take
   (D) to be taken   (   )

9. Tom almost never studied while he was at college, _____ ?

   (A) didn't he
   (B) did he
   (C) wasn't he
   (D) was he   (   )

10. It's time that Jack _____ a driver's license.

   (A) gotten
   (B) got
   (C) getting
   (D) to get   (   )

TEST 24

Directions: *Of the four choices given after each sentence, choose the one most suitable for filling in the blank.*

1. He is _____ telling lies.

   (A) on
   (B) at
   (C) from
   (D) above   (   )

2. If you need reference books, I can lend you _____.

   (A) it
   (B) them
   (C) ones
   (D) some   (   )

3. Although I am busy, I still _____ some shopping.

   (A) make
   (B) do
   (C) go
   (D) buy   (   )

4. I don't think it will happen, but if it _____, I won't know what to do.

   (A) were
   (B) will
   (C) had
   (D) should   (   )

5. Mary, _____ at the sight of the accident, couldn't talk for a while.

   (A) shocked
   (B) shocking
   (C) was shocked
   (D) having shocked   (   )

6. I think you have the _____ number. This is 2704-5525.
   (A) bad
   (B) different
   (C) strange
   (D) wrong   (   )

7. Don't leave your baggage _____ at any time.
   (A) unattends
   (B) no attend
   (C) unattended
   (D) not attending   (   )

8. He said he would lend me the money if I needed it, and he was
   as _____ as his word.
   (A) similar
   (B) better
   (C) good
   (D) harsh   (   )

9. Please forgive me _____ to you in a long time.
   (A) not to write
   (B) not for writing
   (C) for not writing
   (D) not to writing   (   )

10. _____ another aspirin if you still have a headache.
   (A) To try to take
   (B) Try to take
   (C) To try taking
   (D) Try taking   (   )

TEST 25

Directions: *Of the four choices given after each sentence, choose the one most suitable for filling in the blank.*

1. My husband has three sisters; they are my _____.
   - (A) sister-in-laws
   - (B) sister-in-law
   - (C) sisters-in-law
   - (D) sisters-in-laws   (   )

2. We have reached the certainty _____ the meeting will be successful.
   - (A) that
   - (B) which
   - (C) if
   - (D) what   (   )

3. The number of students who came up with some answer or other _____ small.
   - (A) was
   - (B) were
   - (C) have been
   - (D) being   (   )

4. I know the author only _____ name.
   - (A) by
   - (B) for
   - (C) of
   - (D) in   (   )

5. I work _____: Monday, Wednesday, and Friday.
   - (A) every day
   - (B) one another day
   - (C) every other day
   - (D) every two other days   (   )

6. _____ from a distance, his house looked like a matchbox.

   (A) Seen
   (B) Seeing
   (C) To see
   (D) Having seen   (   )

7. Not a _____ of the people were suffering from the food poisoning.

   (A) little
   (B) few
   (C) quite
   (D) number   (   )

8. He went to Vienna with a view _____ music.

   (A) of studying
   (B) in studying
   (C) to studying
   (D) to study   (   )

9. She cannot _____ weep at the bad news.

   (A) to
   (B) but
   (C) help
   (D) be to   (   )

10. Two _____ men who saved the child were praised by everyone.

   (A) brave young American
   (B) young brave American
   (C) American young brave
   (D) brave American young   (   )

TEST 26

Directions: *Of the four choices given after each sentence, choose the one most suitable for filling in the blank.*

1. This car needs _____.

    (A) to repair
    (B) repairing
    (C) having repaired
    (D) being repaired   (   )

2. Mrs. White loves to watch the face of her _____ baby.

    (A) asleep
    (B) sleep
    (C) sleeping
    (D) slept   (   )

3. I don't like cats and my brother doesn't, _____.

    (A) too
    (B) also
    (C) either
    (D) neither   (   )

4. _____ 1100 people live on each square mile of land in that country.

    (A) Many
    (B) So many
    (C) As many as
    (D) So much as   (   )

5. I can't stand _____ any longer.

    (A) that his nasty attitude
    (B) his that nasty attitude
    (C) his nasty attitude of that
    (D) that nasty attitude of his   (   )

6. I would like to make _____ with someone from another country.

   (A) friend
   (B) friends
   (C) a friend
   (D) friendly   (   )

7. The hospital has two spare beds on the second floor, _____ has been used for years. You are welcome to use either one of them.

   (A) both of which
   (B) one of which
   (C) all of which
   (D) neither of which   (   )

8. The rumor passed from mouth to mouth _____ he was alive somewhere in the mountains.

   (A) which
   (B) what
   (C) that
   (D) however   (   )

9. Life changes constantly. Change will always be _____ us.

   (A) besides
   (B) doing
   (C) happening
   (D) with   (   )

10. In America a number of parents _____ angry and worried about guns easily falling into the hands of their children.

   (A) is
   (B) are
   (C) who is
   (D) who are   (   )

TEST 27

Directions: *Of the four choices given after each sentence, choose the one most suitable for filling in the blank.*

1. The reason I could not attend the meeting yesterday was _____ I had a severe headache.

   (A) that
   (B) as
   (C) why
   (D) what   (   )

2. _____ if she should know this?

   (A) How
   (B) What
   (C) Which
   (D) Who   (   )

3. The man decided to wait at the station until his wife _____.

   (A) came
   (B) come
   (C) has come
   (D) will come   (   )

4. "Where has she gone?" "How _____ I know?"

   (A) could
   (B) might
   (C) should
   (D) shall   (   )

5. Although he knows nothing about electronics, he speaks _____ an expert.

   (A) like his being
   (B) as if he were
   (C) even if he were
   (D) as though being   (   )

6. The victim is thought _____ a large quantity of poison by mistake.

    (A) to take
    (B) to have taken
    (C) to be taken
    (D) to have been taken   (   )

7. We didn't _____ to leave Mary out of the plan. It was simply an oversight.

    (A) forget
    (B) mean
    (C) neglect
    (D) seem   (   )

8. This problem is too simple, so it _____.

    (A) is hardly worth discussing
    (B) does hardly worth discussing
    (C) is hardly worth to discuss
    (D) does hardly worthy to discuss   (   )

9. He always stays in bed _____ as he can.

    (A) as lately
    (B) so lately
    (C) as late
    (D) so late   (   )

10. He found five mistakes _____ lines.

    (A) in as many
    (B) like so many
    (C) at so many
    (D) as many as   (   )

TEST 28

Directions: *Of the four choices given after each sentence, choose the one most suitable for filling in the blank.*

1. We shook _____ and parted at the end of our journey.

    (A) arm
    (B) arms
    (C) hands
    (D) hand   (   )

2. It's nice if a child can have _____.

    (A) a room of himself
    (B) a room of his own
    (C) his only room
    (D) a room of his   (   )

3. _____ happens, you may rely on my friendship.

    (A) Whenever
    (B) However
    (C) Whatever
    (D) Whoever   (   )

4. My uncle broke his promise to take us to the beach. _____ my sister was disappointed, her face didn't show it.

    (A) Even
    (B) However
    (C) If
    (D) Then   (   )

5. His clinic _____ many patients since the scandal.

    (A) loses
    (B) has lost
    (C) is losing
    (D) is lost   (   )

6. Extra police _____ to the scene of the trouble.

    (A) was sent
    (B) were sent
    (C) has been sent
    (D) has sent   (   )

7. Mary scarcely seems to care for me, _____?

    (A) does not she
    (B) doesn't she
    (C) does she
    (D) does she not   (   )

8. "What would it cost to _____ this chair repaired?"
"I'd estimate sixty to seventy dollars."

    (A) make
    (B) have
    (C) let
    (D) allow   (   )

9. I never expected that she _____ us.

    (A) joins
    (B) will join
    (C) would join
    (D) has joined   (   )

10. No matter who _____ come, you must not open the door.

    (A) must
    (B) ought
    (C) may
    (D) are   (   )

TEST 29

Directions: *Of the four choices given after each sentence, choose the one most suitable for filling in the blank.*

1. They are very proud of _____ students of that college.
   - (A) being
   - (B) to be
   - (C) being not
   - (D) not to be   (   )

2. Let's stop _____ a cup of coffee and take a rest.
   - (A) that have
   - (B) to be having
   - (C) to have
   - (D) having   (   )

3. You must remember _____ him all that you know, when you see him next.
   - (A) telling
   - (B) having told
   - (C) to tell
   - (D) to be told   (   )

4. "Look at this old coin you have here." "It looks rather old, but I don't know whether it's _____ much."
   - (A) excellent
   - (B) worth
   - (C) valuable
   - (D) useful   (   )

5. I'm going to stop her _____ doing that again.
   - (A) ever
   - (B) never
   - (C) once
   - (D) yet   (   )

6. Like _____ stars among the leaves and branches, the street lamps shed their light.

   (A) very many
   (B) some many
   (C) too many
   (D) so many   (   )

7. They drove to San Francisco taking _____ at the wheel.

   (A) changes
   (B) places
   (C) rides
   (D) turns   (   )

8. They had games, made good friends, and enjoyed _____ very much.

   (A) time
   (B) there
   (C) them
   (D) themselves   (   )

9. New York is the city _____ I have long wanted to visit.

   (A) where
   (B) which
   (C) what
   (D) who   (   )

10. We must admit that there are still many things whose worth cannot be expressed _____ money.

    (A) in part for
    (B) in exchange for
    (C) in favor for
    (D) in terms of   (   )

TEST 30

Directions: *Of the four choices given after each sentence, choose the one most suitable for filling in the blank.*

1. Today's high temperature set a new record. It's extremely hot _____ this time of the year.

    (A) for
    (B) on
    (C) in
    (D) about   (   )

2. _____ grazing in the field.

    (A) A cattle was
    (B) A herd of cattles was
    (C) Cattle were
    (D) Cattles were   (   )

3. The Government ordered that the price of household soap _____ reduced by two pence.

    (A) be
    (B) is
    (C) had been
    (D) can be   (   )

4. This is the best book that I have _____ read.

    (A) once
    (B) ever
    (C) never
    (D) still   (   )

5. You had better _____ your hair cut.

    (A) had
    (B) have
    (C) to get
    (D) to have   (   )

6. He spoke _____ he knew all about our plans when in fact he knew nothing about them.

   (A) that
   (B) as though
   (C) even though
   (D) although   (   )

7. John and Mary _____ meet us at the airport.

   (A) are have to
   (B) are to
   (C) will to
   (D) will be going to   (   )

8. Have you ever tried _____ on the river?

   (A) skate
   (B) skating
   (C) to be skating
   (D) to have skated   (   )

9. She is rather _____ at tennis.

   (A) short
   (B) low
   (C) small
   (D) poor   (   )

10. The money will be divided _____ between the two of them.

   (A) evenly
   (B) sharply
   (C) flatly
   (D) commonly   (   )

TEST 31

Directions: *Of the four choices given after each sentence, choose the one most suitable for filling in the blank.*

1. Sunlight is no _____ necessary to good health than fresh air.

   (A) more
   (B) better
   (C) further
   (D) less   (   )

2. After a hard argument we weren't on speaking _____.

   (A) moods
   (B) connections
   (C) terms
   (D) circles   (   )

3. He was patience _____.

   (A) all
   (B) at all
   (C) itself
   (D) himself   (   )

4. This is the reason for _____ he did it.

   (A) why
   (B) what
   (C) which
   (D) that   (   )

5. You won't be able to reach the airport in time _____ you drive faster.

   (A) unless
   (B) if
   (C) even
   (D) if not   (   )

6. What is the weather in your hometown _____ about this time
   of the year?

   (A) likely
   (B) like
   (C) liked
   (D) alike   (   )

7. He is the man _____ I believe can help you.

   (A) as
   (B) who
   (C) whom
   (D) whomever   (   )

8. _____ is no telling how long their quarrel will last.

   (A) He
   (B) One
   (C) There
   (D) This   (   )

9. We _____ attend the meeting.

   (A) had no better
   (B) had better not
   (C) not had better
   (D) had not better to   (   )

10. Look! What a beautiful house! How I wish I _____ a house
    like that.

   (A) could buy
   (B) can buy
   (C) have bought
   (D) can have bought   (   )

TEST 32

Directions: *Of the four choices given after each sentence, choose the one most suitable for filling in the blank.*

1. You are _____ here by midnight, or you'll get punished.

   (A) return
   (B) being returned
   (C) returned
   (D) to return   (   )

2. His mother has been _____ a drugstore for fifteen years.

   (A) running
   (B) having
   (C) taking
   (D) making   (   )

3. We had to drive very slowly _____ fog.

   (A) instead of
   (B) according to
   (C) by means of
   (D) on account of   (   )

4. His work is _____ satisfactory and therefore, he has been asked to do it over again.

   (A) far from
   (B) a little bit
   (C) very much
   (D) extremely   (   )

5. I've already had one bad experience buying goods by mail order and I don't want _____.

   (A) another
   (B) any longer
   (C) at all
   (D) other   (   )

6. The boy took great _____ to try to work out the problem.

   (A) effects
   (B) struggles
   (C) senses
   (D) pains   (   )

7. She went _____ to say that he was a swindler.

   (A) too far
   (B) so far as
   (C) so long as
   (D) too long   (   )

8. The bomb fell within about twenty paces of _____ we had been sitting.

   (A) which
   (B) the place of
   (C) what
   (D) where   (   )

9. This dish looks terrible! I wouldn't eat it _____ I were starving.

   (A) after
   (B) because
   (C) even if
   (D) only when

10. If people become sleepy when they read good books, it is _____ they are unwilling to make the effort, _____ they do not know how to make it.

   (A) not because ; but because
   (B) not as ; but as
   (C) either ; or
   (D) neither ; nor   (   ).

TEST 33

Directions: *Of the four choices given after each sentence, choose the one most suitable for filling in the blank.*

1. _____ white, this house looks bigger.

   (A) Paint
   (B) Painting
   (C) Painted
   (D) To paint   (   )

2. He couldn't get the car _____ and went by bus.

   (A) start
   (B) to start
   (C) started
   (D) be started   (   )

3. The students played _____ on April Fools' Day.

   (A) to their teacher a trick
   (B) their teacher a trick
   (C) their teacher at a trick
   (D) their teacher by a trick   (   )

4. No matter what you _____ me to do, I'll do it.

   (A) hope
   (B) have
   (C) wish
   (D) make   (   )

5. The American consumer is more and more interested in food that has no artificial ingredients _____ to it.

   (A) added
   (B) adding
   (C) having added
   (D) to add   (   )

6. David is an honest boy. His honest deed is _____ praised.

    (A) worth
    (B) worth of
    (C) worthy to be
    (D) worthy of   (   )

7. Richard studied so hard _____ well on the test.

    (A) that he had not done
    (B) that he should not have done
    (C) that he must have done
    (D) that he had to be done   (   )

8. The play was a lot of fun. I wish you _____ there.

    (A) could be
    (B) could have been
    (C) have been
    (D) would be   (   )

9. You only started this job an hour ago; surely you _____ it, have you?

    (A) finished
    (B) have finished
    (C) haven't been finished
    (D) haven't finished   (   )

10. The English of this composition is too good. She can't _____ it herself.

    (A) have to write
    (B) have written
    (C) had written
    (D) be written   (   )

TEST 34

Directions: *Of the four choices given after each sentence, choose the one most suitable for filling in the blank.*

1. How lonely and helpless she must feel left all _____!

   (A) over the world
   (B) the more
   (C) work and no play
   (D) by herself   (   )

2. Pat is very talkative. This is _____ I don't like him.

   (A) what
   (B) why
   (C) that
   (D) because   (   )

3. Let's get going in case the bus _____ early.

   (A) doesn't leave
   (B) leaves
   (C) will leave
   (D) won't leave   (   )

4. On such a hot day, I prefer _____ at home _____ out.

   (A) stay ; to go
   (B) staying ; to going
   (C) to stay ; than to go
   (D) staying ; than going   (   )

5. It struck me as strange _____ my front door was open when I got home.

   (A) which
   (B) as
   (C) what
   (D) that   (   )

6. I _____ to Italy, though I've always wanted to go.

    (A) have been

    (B) have never been

    (C) had never gone

    (D) had gone   ( )

7. She was _____ than angry when her son lied again.

    (A) sader

    (B) sadder

    (C) more sad

    (D) much sad   ( )

8. A famous cellist _____ from Germany will give a recital tonight.

    (A) returned

    (B) returning

    (C) being returned

    (D) having returning   ( )

9. Do you know that Japan once produced more silk than _____ country?

    (A) different

    (B) other

    (C) another

    (D) any other   ( )

10. He was one of the famous men of _____ of his time.

    (A) book

    (B) writings

    (C) letters

    (D) papers   ( )

TEST 35

Directions: *Of the four choices given after each sentence, choose the one most suitable for filling in the blank.*

1. He will return the book as soon as he _____ with it.

   (A) will do
   (B) has done
   (C) will have done
   (D) will be done   (   )

2. The river is very dangerous _____.

   (A) to swim
   (B) swim
   (C) to swim in
   (D) swim in   (   )

3. _____ more pleasant than traveling.

   (A) Nothing is
   (B) Another thing is not
   (C) Anything is not
   (D) Not at all   (   )

4. _____ I admit that the problem is difficult, I still believe it is solvable.

   (A) If
   (B) While
   (C) Because
   (D) Despite   (   )

5. Dark _____ it was, we managed to find our way home.

   (A) after
   (B) although
   (C) as
   (D) before   (   )

6. A large proportion of _____ English-speaking people watch on TV is of American origin.

   (A) that
   (B) what
   (C) where
   (D) which   (   )

7. As I was invited to the party, I was _____ myself with pleasure.

   (A) at
   (B) beside
   (C) for
   (D) over   (   )

8. Water turns _____ ice at 32 °F.

   (A) off
   (B) out
   (C) up
   (D) into   (   )

9. It was a terrifying experience to _____ the world rocking during the earthquake.

   (A) feel
   (B) fall
   (C) fell
   (D) felt   (   )

10. I've never heard you are in this town. How long _____?

    (A) are you here
    (B) had you been here
    (C) were you here
    (D) have you been here   (   )

TEST 36

Directions: *Of the four choices given after each sentence, choose the one most suitable for filling in the blank.*

1. She has not come here yet. I am afraid she _____ her way.

    (A) may be lost
    (B) may have lost
    (C) may be having lost
    (D) may have been lost   (   )

2. If _____ I could speak English as fluently as you!

    (A) not
    (B) so be
    (C) only
    (D) merely   (   )

3. She is very frugal, not to _____ stingy.

    (A) remark
    (B) say
    (C) speak
    (D) tell   (   )

4. A serious illness _____ him to drop out of school.

    (A) made
    (B) let
    (C) had
    (D) caused   (   )

5. It was very sensible _____ him to reject the bribe.

    (A) to
    (B) of
    (C) with
    (D) about   (   )

6. _____ beautiful roses you sent me! It was nice of you.

   (A) How
   (B) What
   (C) Which
   (D) That   (   )

7. At _____ time in my life have I been busier than I am today.

   (A) any
   (B) no
   (C) other
   (D) some   (   )

8. Next to my house lives a _____ teacher.

   (A) retire
   (B) retiring
   (C) retired
   (D) retirement   (   )

9. I burst out laughing _____ myself.

   (A) regardless of
   (B) in spite of
   (C) forgetting about
   (D) against   (   )

10. He said he couldn't speak Russian, _____ was untrue.

   (A) which
   (B) what
   (C) why
   (D) how   (   )

TEST 37

Directions: *Of the four choices given after each sentence, choose the one most suitable for filling in the blank.*

1. She was able to go to college _____ the scholarship.

    (A) to
    (B) in
    (C) according to
    (D) thanks to   (   )

2. _____ all the magazines on the shelf, there was one that was very interesting.

    (A) Among
    (B) By
    (C) Between
    (D) From   (   )

3. He said that his uncle _____ to see him the night before.

    (A) had come
    (B) came
    (C) has come
    (D) will come   (   )

4. I'm sure I _____ her two years ago.

    (A) have seen
    (B) saw
    (C) will have seen
    (D) had seen   (   )

5. _____ that our father were here to help us!

    (A) Would
    (B) May
    (C) Could
    (D) Should   (   )

6. You _____ such a large house. Your wife would have been quite happy in a smaller house.

    (A) need not buy

    (B) needn't have bought

    (C) will need to buy

    (D) needed to buy   (   )

7. If you go near a camel, you risk _____.

    (A) bitten

    (B) is bitten

    (C) being bitten

    (D) having bitten   (   )

8. What sort of curtains do you think should _____ with the carpet?

    (A) go

    (B) fit

    (C) suit

    (D) match   (   )

9. It's a long time since I saw him _____.

    (A) later

    (B) latter

    (C) last

    (D) latest   (   )

10. Lost things have a way of appearing when _____ expected.

    (A) best

    (B) least

    (C) worst

    (D) most   (   )

TEST 38

Directions: *Of the four choices given after each sentence, choose the one most suitable for filling in the blank.*

1. As a statesman, Churchill was more successful than _____ I ever knew.

    (A) everyone
    (B) each one
    (C) anyone
    (D) no one   (   )

2. She is a lady, and will be treated _____.

    (A) as that
    (B) as such
    (C) like such
    (D) to such   (   )

3. The doctor decided to operate at once. The patient's condition _____ no delay.

    (A) allowed of
    (B) allowed for
    (C) thought of
    (D) thought about   (   )

4. _____ writer has dealt with the topic of "life and death."

    (A) Many
    (B) A lot of
    (C) Many a
    (D) A number of   (   )

5. I am wondering _____.

    (A) which house this belongs to
    (B) which house belongs to this
    (C) whose house this is
    (D) whose house is this   (   )

6. Pollution has reached _____ great an extent that we are barely able to cope with it.

    (A)   much
    (B)   many
    (C)   so
    (D)   such   (   )

7. When she saw all her children safe at home, her delight was _____ that she could not speak a word.

    (A)   so
    (B)   such
    (C)   very much
    (D)   great   (   )

8. He gave me clear directions and so I had no trouble _____ his office.

    (A)   find
    (B)   found
    (C)   finding
    (D)   to find   (   )

9. I _____ you last night, but I was too busy.

    (A)   had to telephone
    (B)   must have telephoned
    (C)   should have telephoned
    (D)   should telephone   (   )

10. Some day or _____ you will regret it.

    (A)   another
    (B)   ones
    (C)   other
    (D)   second   (   )

TEST 39

Directions: Of the four choices given after each sentence, choose the one most suitable for filling in the blank.

1. I'm _____ excited to eat anything.

   (A) enough
   (B) hardly
   (C) much
   (D) too   (   )

2. Did the newspaper _____ it was going to rain?

   (A) say
   (B) talk
   (C) tell
   (D) write   (   )

3. After his explanation, she did not understand but became more _____.

   (A) confused
   (B) confusing
   (C) understanding
   (D) considerable   (   )

4. His theory is very difficult; _____ people understand it.

   (A) little
   (B) a little
   (C) few
   (D) a few   (   )

5. _____ at home, so their mother is left all alone.

   (A) Either Tom or Mary lives
   (B) Neither Tom nor Mary lives
   (C) Both Tom and Mary live
   (D) Both Tom and Mary don't live   (   )

6. Everyone liked her, and was glad _____ her company.

    (A) having
    (B) have
    (C) to have
    (D) had   (   )

7. The only method I know which will help you remember what
    you have heard at the lecture is _____ of keeping notes.

    (A) some sort
    (B) that
    (C) the manner
    (D) which   (   )

8. Were I wealthy, _____ I'm not, I would still go to work
    every day.

    (A) so
    (B) what
    (C) which
    (D) while   (   )

9. Reluctant as he was, he had no choice _____ to the other
    party's proposal.

    (A) but agreeing
    (B) to agree
    (C) but agree
    (D) but to agree   (   )

10. The thief ran away at the _____ of a policeman.

    (A) screen
    (B) scenery
    (C) sight
    (D) seeing   (   )

TEST 40

Directions: *Of the four choices given after each sentence, choose the one most suitable for filling in the blank.*

1. Among the guests _____ to the party were two foreign ladies.

   (A) invite
   (B) invited
   (C) inviting
   (D) who invited   (   )

2. How long _____ here by the end of next year?

   (A) will you work
   (B) are you working
   (C) you will have worked
   (D) will you have been working   (   )

3. The picture was wonderful. You _____ to have seen it.

   (A) ought
   (B) should
   (C) have
   (D) had   (   )

4. I am very regretful for _____ I said to her yesterday.

   (A) that
   (B) whether
   (C) what
   (D) which   (   )

5. The window was _____ see through.

   (A) enough dirty to
   (B) so dirty that you can
   (C) so dirty to
   (D) too dirty to   (   )

6. Most of the job is complete, but a few things _____ done.

   (A) have remain to be
   (B) remain to be
   (C) are remained to be
   (D) are remaining to be   (   )

7. No doubt Mary is wrong, but I would rather _____ too much, since nobody is perfect.

   (A) you not to pick on her
   (B) you didn't pick on her
   (C) you not picking on her
   (D) you don't pick on her   (   )

8. My students were few in number, _____ four or five altogether.

   (A) as many as
   (B) as little as
   (C) no less than
   (D) no more than   (   )

9. The next train will be _____ crowded than this one.

   (A) much
   (B) a little
   (C) as
   (D) less   (   )

10. I saw two tall figures _____ slowly in the dusk.

   (A) walked
   (B) to walk
   (C) walking
   (D) be walking   (   )

TEST 41

Directions: *Of the four choices given after each sentence, choose the one most suitable for filling in the blank.*

1. Changes have taken place in many areas of our life, especially in _____ related to housing and employment.

   (A) it
   (B) that
   (C) these
   (D) those   (   )

2. _____ of a novelist, he has the ability to make acute observations of people.

   (A) As may be expected
   (B) Judging
   (C) As a viewpoint
   (D) Viewing   (   )

3. My sister _____ here by now, for she took the early train.

   (A) must arrive
   (B) can arrive
   (C) may arrive
   (D) ought to have arrived   (   )

4. He wanted to succeed even at the _____ of his health.

   (A) danger
   (B) service
   (C) expense
   (D) mercy   (   )

5. It is yet _____ whether this plan will succeed or not.

   (A) impossible
   (B) unfinished
   (C) much to do
   (D) to be seen   (   )

6. Please return the book when you _____ reading it.
   - (A) finished
   - (B) had finished
   - (C) will finish
   - (D) have finished   (   )

7. I don't mind lending you the money _____ you pay it back within a year.
   - (A) which
   - (B) supposed
   - (C) whether
   - (D) provided   (   )

8. _____ for the support of the public, the President could not have survived the revolt.
   - (A) But
   - (B) If it were
   - (C) Unless
   - (D) Without   (   )

9. He is so wise that he knows better.
   = He is _____ wise not to know better.
   - (A) enough
   - (B) so
   - (C) too
   - (D) very   (   )

10. He kissed the lady _____ the hand to show his respect.
    - (A) on
    - (B) by
    - (C) at
    - (D) with   (   )

TEST 42

Directions: *Of the four choices given after each sentence, choose the one most suitable for filling in the blank.*

1. These part-timers are paid _____ hour.

   (A) in the
   (B) in an
   (C) by the
   (D) by an   (   )

2. Philosophy is not _____ as you imagine it is.

   (A) so difficult subject
   (B) so a difficult subject
   (C) a so difficult subject
   (D) so difficult a subject   (   )

3. John is _____ of the two boys.

   (A) taller
   (B) the taller
   (C) tallest
   (D) the tallest   (   )

4. He is a great inventor and is called _____ of the age.

   (A) Edisons
   (B) an Edison
   (C) the Edison
   (D) Edison   (   )

5. _____ who insults himself will be insulted by others.

   (A) That
   (B) He
   (C) Those
   (D) Which   (   )

6. You can borrow two books _____ condition that you bring them back within a week.

(A) at
(B) with
(C) by
(D) on   (   )

7. In the park, _____ sat on benches and others strolled about.

(A) boys
(B) many
(C) people
(D) some   (   )

8. Farmers are always _____ the weather.

(A) at the mercy of
(B) depended on
(C) dependent in
(D) merciful of   (   )

9. After a long walk in the sun, I was overcome _____.

(A) with the thirst
(B) with thirsty
(C) by the thirst
(D) by thirsty   (   )

10. I _____ reading for an hour when he came in.

(A) was
(B) have been
(C) had been
(D) will be   (   )

TEST 43

Directions: *Of the four choices given after each sentence, choose the one most suitable for filling in the blank.*

1. We have plenty of bread, so I _____ buy a loaf.

    (A) needn't to
    (B) must not
    (C) haven't to
    (D) don't need to   (   )

2. As the summer vacation nears, I'm looking forward _____ my friends.

    (A) to meet
    (B) to meeting
    (C) for meeting
    (D) to be meeting   (   )

3. The wall wasn't _____ dogs out.

    (A) high enough to keep
    (B) so high as keep
    (C) higher than to keep
    (D) so high that can keep   (   )

4. You are _____ to gain weight in summer than in winter because you tend to lose your appetite when it is hot.

    (A) less likely
    (B) less unlikely
    (C) very likely
    (D) very unlikely   (   )

5. _____ are very sociable people. They love to give parties very often.

    (A) The Johnson
    (B) Johnson
    (C) The Johnsons
    (D) Johnsons   (   )

6. Come over and see me _____ tomorrow.

   (A) sometime
   (B) some time
   (C) sometimes
   (D) some times   (   )

7. My father _____ that we should go camping.

   (A) invited
   (B) talked
   (C) told
   (D) suggested   (   )

8. Judy _____ me that she would come to our party tonight.

   (A) said
   (B) spoke
   (C) talked
   (D) told   (   )

9. Study is necessary, and so is practice. The combination will give
   one the ability to communicate in a foreign language, but _____
   will result in slow, incorrect speech.

   (A) all of them
   (B) both of them
   (C) none of them
   (D) either one of them alone   (   )

10. We honor him for _____ he is, not for _____ he has.

   (A) that
   (B) what
   (C) which
   (D) how   (   )

TEST 44

Directions: *Of the four choices given after each sentence, choose the one most suitable for filling in the blank.*

1. _____ he is wealthy, he is not content.

   (A) With all
   (B) For all
   (C) In spite of
   (D) Despite   (   )

2. The teacher as well as the students _____ to study hard.

   (A) are expected
   (B) expected
   (C) expect
   (D) is expected   (   )

3. Billiards _____ a good and interesting indoor game.

   (A) is
   (B) are
   (C) has
   (D) have   (   )

4. When I get home, my wife will probably _____ television.

   (A) have been watched
   (B) watched
   (C) watch
   (D) be watching   (   )

5. It is a pity that he _____ miss such a good opportunity.

   (A) could
   (B) should
   (C) would
   (D) must   (   )

6. We _____ Tom honest.

   (A) see
   (B) expect
   (C) regard
   (D) consider   (   )

7. The wind was not _____ to prevent us from sky-diving.

   (A) as strong
   (B) as strong as
   (C) so strong
   (D) so strong as   (   )

8. The guests _____ the happy couple a long and prosperous life.

   (A) hoped
   (B) wanted
   (C) supposed
   (D) wished   (   )

9. It was at the bookstore _____ I met my future wife.

   (A) which
   (B) that
   (C) this
   (D) here   (   )

10. The train makes several stops _____ Taipei and Taichung.

   (A) between
   (B) from
   (C) among
   (D) beside   (   )

TEST 45

Directions: *Of the four choices given after each sentence, choose the one most suitable for filling in the blank.*

1. Science is far _____ a collection of facts and methods.

    (A) away from
    (B) down from
    (C) less as
    (D) more than   (   )

2. He is _____ of a musician.

    (A) anybody
    (B) anything
    (C) somebody
    (D) something   (   )

3. The hairdresser now cuts _____ men's and women's hair.

    (A) either
    (B) both
    (C) each
    (D) any   (   )

4. He is _____ is called a self-made man.

    (A) that
    (B) which
    (C) what
    (D) who   (   )

5. Living _____ I do so remote from town, I rarely meet people.

    (A) where
    (B) as
    (C) while
    (D) if   (   )

6. The train was running _____ full speed.

    (A) at

    (B) with

    (C) by

    (D) in   (   )

7. _____ present at the meeting supported the bill.

    (A) These

    (B) That

    (C) Those

    (D) They   (   )

8. His warning _____ by the villagers.

    (A) was paid no attention

    (B) was paid no attention to

    (C) paid no attention

    (D) paid no attention to   (   )

9. It is necessary that every member _____ acquaint himself with the rules of the club as soon as possible.

    (A) would

    (B) might

    (C) should

    (D) could   (   )

10. He did his best; otherwise he _____ the first prize.

    (A) cannot win

    (B) would have won

    (C) will not have won

    (D) would not have won   (   )

TEST 46

Directions: *Of the four choices given after each sentence, choose the one most suitable for filling in the blank.*

1. His beard made him look older _____ ten years.

    (A) by
    (B) with
    (C) to
    (D) in   (   )

2. Spaghetti and meat sauce _____ one of my favorite dishes.

    (A) are
    (B) is
    (C) were
    (D) be   (   )

3. She was seen _____ the room.

    (A) enter
    (B) entered
    (C) be entered
    (D) to enter   (   )

4. His salary is _____ what it was seven years ago.

    (A) double
    (B) as double
    (C) by double
    (D) for double   (   )

5. You can't vote _____ you have satisfied all the formal conditions.

    (A) until
    (B) when
    (C) whenever
    (D) since   (   )

6. Only after the accident _____ have his car inspected.

   (A) had he
   (B) he had
   (C) did he
   (D) he did   (   )

7. Science as _____ is not primarily interested in the value or worth of things.

   (A) itself
   (B) known
   (C) seen
   (D) such   (   )

8. She studied hard with a _____ to becoming a teacher of Japanese.

   (A) means
   (B) purpose
   (C) hope
   (D) view   (   )

9. I was not in the _____ surprised at what he said.

   (A) last
   (B) all
   (C) least
   (D) latest   (   )

10. It has been _____ hot these days.

   (A) steam
   (B) steaming
   (C) steamed
   (D) steamy   (   )

TEST 47

Directions: *Of the four choices given after each sentence, choose the one most suitable for filling in the blank.*

1. _____ the recent political corruption, the minister had to resign.

   (A) As
   (B) As a result
   (C) Because
   (D) Because of   (   )

2. By the age of 25, she _____ in five different countries.

   (A) has lived
   (B) had lived
   (C) lives
   (D) lived   (   )

3. My father insisted I _____ go to see the place.

   (A) might
   (B) ought
   (C) should
   (D) would   (   )

4. We make cotton _____ many useful things.

   (A) of
   (B) out of
   (C) into
   (D) from   (   )

5. It is no _____ arguing about it, because he will never change his mind.

   (A) use
   (B) help
   (C) time
   (D) while   (   )

6. There _____ no bus service, I had to take a taxi.

   (A) is
   (B) be
   (C) being
   (D) been   (   )

7. "Would you pass me the salt?" "_____."

   (A) Here are you
   (B) Here you are
   (C) Here is it
   (D) Here are they   (   )

8. Let's go to the movies together, _____?

   (A) shall we
   (B) will you
   (C) don't we
   (D) won't you   (   )

9. This vacuum cleaner is highly recommended for _____ durability.

   (A) its
   (B) it's
   (C) it is
   (D) that   (   )

10. Tom and Joe look alike. I always mistake one _____ the other.

   (A) from
   (B) with
   (C) of
   (D) for   (   )

TEST 48

Directions: *Of the four choices given after each sentence, choose the one most suitable for filling in the blank.*

1. "Do you think we'll have good weather?"
   "I hope _____."
   (A) for
   (B) it
   (C) so
   (D) to   (   )

2. There is no rule _____ has exceptions.
   (A) but
   (B) that
   (C) without
   (D) which   (   )

3. I'll have returned to America _____ this letter reaches you.
   (A) if
   (B) until
   (C) by the time
   (D) now that   (   )

4. He bought a new camera _____ two hundred dollars.
   (A) by
   (B) for
   (C) in
   (D) with   (   )

5. This machine did not function properly when it was delivered to my house. It _____ broken during shipping.
   (A) can have
   (B) could be
   (C) has to be
   (D) must have been   (   )

6. "Tomorrow our professor is going back to England."
   "I didn't know he _____."

   (A) had decided to leave
   (B) would have decided to leave
   (C) will decide to leave
   (D) is deciding to leave   (   )

7. Sarah demanded that she _____ given a refund.

   (A) is
   (B) be
   (C) will be
   (D) need be   (   )

8. My husband is an expert when it comes _____ Chinese food.

   (A) to cook
   (B) to cooking
   (C) of cooking
   (D) for cooking   (   )

9. The audience could not but _____ the performance of the pianist.

   (A) admire
   (B) to admire
   (C) admired
   (D) admiring   (   )

10. Will this much food _____ for a week's camping?

    (A) do
    (B) enough
    (C) all right
    (D) content   (   )

TEST 49

Directions: *Of the four choices given after each sentence, choose the one most suitable for filling in the blank.*

1. _____ students as Joe and Don need more encouragement from the teachers.

    (A) So
    (B) Such
    (C) Like
    (D) For example   (   )

2. In case of emergency, leave the building as quickly as possible _____.

    (A) if instructed otherwise
    (B) so instructed otherwise
    (C) but otherwise instructed
    (D) unless otherwise instructed   (   )

3. Her mother was busy _____ the dinner at that time.

    (A) cooking
    (B) to cook
    (C) in cook
    (D) for cooking   (   )

4. _____ are you moving the furniture for?

    (A) What
    (B) How
    (C) Where
    (D) Why   (   )

5. I may have to work, _____ I'll call you.

    (A) for which
    (B) in which case
    (C) whereby
    (D) wherefore   (   )

6. "Is Mary coming today?" "I _____. She is sick."

   (A) don't suppose

   (B) suppose her not

   (C) suppose not

   (D) don't suppose her to   (   )

7. The trouble is, _____ we get used to watching TV, we gradually come to watch it more and more.

   (A) what

   (B) so

   (C) that

   (D) once   (   )

8. It is high time that we _____ immediate action to solve the problem.

   (A) took

   (B) take

   (C) must take

   (D) to take   (   )

9. You can wear my scarf _____ you don't spill anything on it.

   (A) as long as

   (B) unless

   (C) even if

   (D) so that   (   )

10. It used to be difficult to enter university, but it is much easier than _____ now.

   (A) any

   (B) ever

   (C) never

   (D) once   (   )

TEST 50

Directions: *Of the four choices given after each sentence, choose the one most suitable for filling in the blank.*

1. The pale look on his face suggested that he _____ afraid.

   (A) is
   (B) was
   (C) be
   (D) had been   (   )

2. What do you say _____ a cup of coffee?

   (A) to have
   (B) about having
   (C) to having
   (D) for having   (   )

3. We could do nothing _____ wait until the next morning.

   (A) as
   (B) but
   (C) that
   (D) with   (   )

4. It's a little cold. Would you mind _____ the window?

   (A) me to close
   (B) to close
   (C) I close
   (D) my closing   (   )

5. The heavy rain kept us _____ out yesterday.

   (A) from going
   (B) into going
   (C) to go
   (D) to be going   (   )

6. My father sat watching TV, _____ our dog, Babe, lying beside him.

   (A) with
   (B) by
   (C) as
   (D) to   (   )

7. We went to the restaurant he recommended, _____ was famous for its lamb chops.

   (A) where
   (B) which
   (C) when
   (D) how   (   )

8. It is such a heavy stone _____ he can't lift.

   (A) whom
   (B) that
   (C) which
   (D) as   (   )

9. _____ tourist naturally wants to see as much as possible of the country he is visiting.

   (A) Any
   (B) Some
   (C) Few
   (D) A lot of   (   )

10. Mr. Smith grew colder and colder _____ finally he got up and left the room.

   (A) as
   (B) than
   (C) until
   (D) whenever   (   )

☆ ☆ ☆ 全國最完整的文法書 ☆ ☆ ☆

文法寶典全集

劉 毅 編著 / 售價990元

　　這是一本想學好英文的人必備的工具書，作者積多年豐富的教學經驗，針對大家所不了解和最容易犯錯的地方，編寫成一本完整的文法書。

　　本書編排方式與眾不同，第一篇就給讀者整體的概念，再詳述文法中的細節部分，內容十分完整。文法說明以圖表為中心，一目了然，並且務求深入淺出。無論您在考試中或其他書中所遇到的任何不了解的問題，或是您感到最煩惱的文法問題，查閱「文法寶典全集」均可迎刃而解。

　　哪些副詞可修飾名詞或代名詞？(P.228)；什麼是介副詞？(P.543)；哪些名詞可以當副詞用？(P.100)；倒裝句(P.629)、省略句(P.644)等特殊構句，為什麼倒裝？為什麼省略？原來的句子是什麼樣子？在「文法寶典全集」裏都有詳盡的說明。

　　可見如果學文法不求徹底了解，反而成為學習英文的絆腳石，只要讀完本書，您必定信心十足，大幅提高對英文的興趣與實力。

跟著百萬網紅「劉毅完美英語」學英文

劉毅老師在「快手」、「抖音」網站，每堂課平均約30秒，每天有2~3堂課，任何時間、任何地點都可以重複練習，在線上從小學、國中、高中、大學到成人，不分年齡、不分程度，人人可學。可和劉毅老師一對一討論，什麼問題都可以問，有問必答！用劉毅老師說的話來留言，寫得愈多，進步愈多，可以輕鬆應付任何考試！

立即掃描QR碼，下載「快手」、「抖音」，搜索「劉毅完美英語」，點讚、分享及關注，成為粉絲，享受免費英語課程！

中級英語文法測驗（學生用書）
Intermediate Level
English Grammar Tests

售價：120元

主　　　編／劉　毅
發　行　所／學習出版有限公司　　☎ (02) 2704-5525
郵 撥 帳 號／ 05127272 學習出版社帳戶
登　記　證／局版台業 2179 號
印　刷　所／文聯彩色印刷有限公司
台 北 門 市／台北市許昌街 17 號 6F　　☎ (02) 2331-4060
台灣總經銷／紅螞蟻圖書有限公司　　☎ (02) 2795-3656
本公司網址／ www.learnbook.com.tw
電 子 郵 件／ learnbook0928@gmail.com

2023 年 11 月 1 日新修訂

ISBN 978-957-519-555-7